W9-CMO-040

# FAST FACTS

# HOT BIKES

## ROLAND BROWN

SEA-TO-SEA

*Mankato Collingwood London*

This edition first published in 2012 by
Sea-to-Sea Publications
Distributed by Black Rabbit Books
P.O. Box 3263, Mankato, Minnesota 56002

Copyright © Sea-to-Sea Publications 2012

Printed in China

All rights reserved.

9 8 7 6 5 4 3 2

Published by arrangement with the Watts Publishing Group Ltd, London.

Library of Congress Cataloging-in-Publication Data

Brown, Roland.
  Hot bikes / by Roland Brown.
     p. cm. -- (Fast facts)
  Includes index.
  ISBN 978-1-59771-326-9 (library binding)
  1. Motorcycles--Juvenile literature. I. Title.
TL440.15.B76 2012
629.227'5--dc22
                        2011001211

Series editor: Adrian Cole
Photographer (unless credited below): Roland Brown Motorcycle Photography
Art director: Jonathan Hair
Design: Blue Paw Design
Picture research: Sophie Hartley
Consultants: Fiona M. Collins and Philippa Hunt, Roehampton University, UK

Acknowledgments:
all photography by Roland Brown Photography except: afaizal/Shutterstock: front cover.
Bo Bridges/Corbis: 24. Hulton Deutsch/Corbis: 7. ITV/Rex Features: 15. Yoav
Lemmer/AFP/Getty Images: 19tr. Claudio Onorati/epa/Corbis: 21. Dean Turner
/istockphoto: front cover background.

February 2011
RD/6000006415/001

   *Every effort has been made by the Publishers to ensure that the web sites in this book contain no inappropriate or offensive material. However, because of the nature of the Internet, it is impossible to guarantee that the contents of these sites will not be altered. We strongly advise that Internet access is supervised by a responsible adult.*

# Contents

*Words that are highlighted appear in the glossary.*

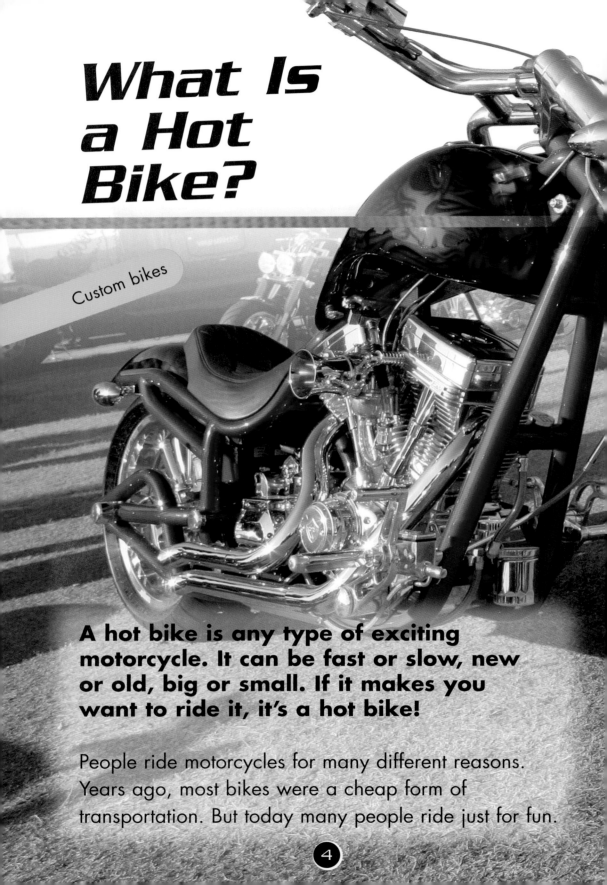

# What Is a Hot Bike?

Custom bikes

**A hot bike is any type of exciting motorcycle. It can be fast or slow, new or old, big or small. If it makes you want to ride it, it's a hot bike!**

People ride motorcycles for many different reasons. Years ago, most bikes were a cheap form of transportation. But today many people ride just for fun.

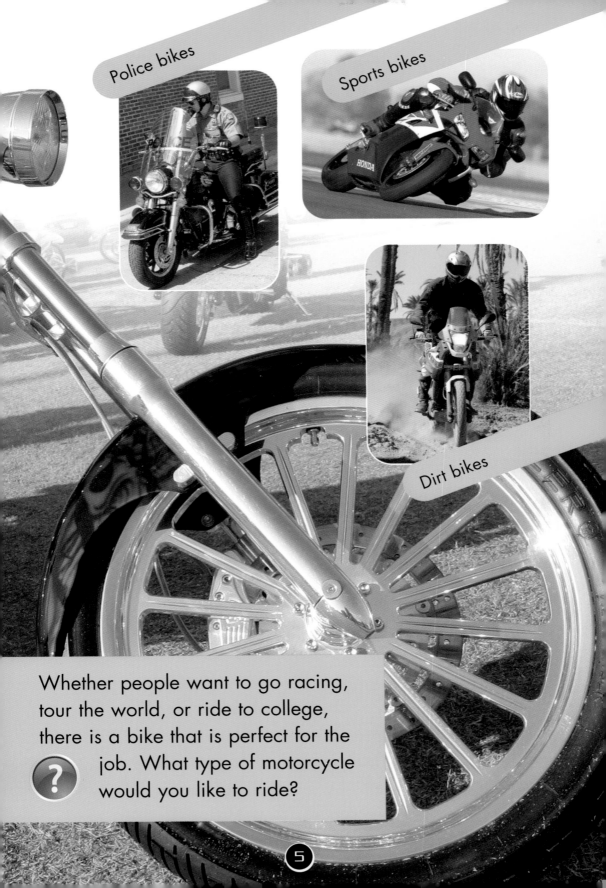

Police bikes

Sports bikes

Dirt bikes

Whether people want to go racing, tour the world, or ride to college, there is a bike that is perfect for the job. What type of motorcycle would you like to ride?

# The Bike Is Born

**The first motorcycle ever was built
in Germany in 1885 by an engineer
called Gottlieb Daimler. It was
made mostly of wood.**

Gottlieb Daimler had a 17-year-old son, Paul. He
was the first to ride the motorcycle, but he had to
stop when the saddle caught fire—a really hot bike!

In 1903, Harley-Davidson was founded by Bill
Harley and the three Davidson brothers from
Milwaukee. They bolted a small engine into a
bicycle frame. Their new motorbike (above)
soon became a big success.

# FF Top Fact

Motorbikes, such as the twin-cylinder Douglas, were used by the British Army to carry messages during World War I (1914–1918).

# FF Record

In 1907, Rem Fowler set a lap record of 43 **mph** (69 **km/h**) in winning the first Isle of Man TT (Tourist Trophy) race ever.

People watching the 1936 Isle of Man TT.

## ONLINE//:

**http://www.iomtt.com**
Check out the famous Isle of Man TT, where motorbikes race on normal roads. Find out about the circuit, the history, and download videos.

# Classics

**Classic bikes are the great machines from the past. They range in age from 15 to more than 100 years old.**

British bikes ruled the roads in the 1950s and 1960s. Models such as the 30.5 cubic inch (500**cc**) Norton Dominator (below) and 40 cubic inch (650cc) Triumph Bonneville were fast and popular.

## FF Record

Triumph's Bonneville was named after the Bonneville dry lake in Utah. That's where, in 1956, a Triumph ridden by Johnny Allen was timed at 214 mph (344 km/h).

Japanese motorcycles took over in the 1970s. **Superbikes,** such as the Honda CB750 (below) and Kawasaki Z900, were more powerful than the British machines. They were also more reliable.

Many classic bike owners enjoy polishing and restoring their old machines, as well as riding them.

**ONLINE//:**

**http://www.harley-davidson.com**
Visit the Museum section of the Harley-Davidson site and go to Online Exhibits for great photos of classic racers.

# Tourers and Cruisers

**Tourers are big, powerful bikes you can ride in comfort over long distances.**

Machines including BMW's K1200LT (below) and Honda's Gold Wing include luxuries, such as heated seats, **saddlebags**, and powerful sound systems.

## *FF* Record

Adventurer Nick Sanders rode his Yamaha around the world in a record 19 days!

Cruisers are long, laid-back bikes, designed more for style than for speed or comfort. Motorcycles such as Harley-Davidson's Rocker (above) have big **V-twin** engines.

## FF Top Fact

Thousands of motorcyclists visit Daytona Beach in Florida during Bike Week every March. They cruise up and down Main Street and on the sandy beach itself.

**?** Which type of bike would you rather ride—tourer or cruiser?

## ONLINE//:

**http://www.edelweissbike.com**
Plan your dream motorcycle trip on touring firm Edelweiss's fab site. Check out the photo albums and route maps.

# Streetfighters

**Streetfighters are the bad boys of motorcycling. They are powerful and fast.**

Most streetfighters have simple, stripped-down styling. Many have twin headlights and **tuned** engines. Streetfighter riders perform **wheelies** and other stunts.

The streetfighter craze began when riders crashed their sports bikes, and didn't replace their broken **fairings**. Later, bike manufacturers produced custom-made streetfighters, such as Honda's CB1000R (above) and Triumph's Speed Triple.

Triumph's Speed Triple is a great stunt bike.

# FF Top Fact

The unfaired V-twin launched by Ducati in 2009 definitely fits into this **class** of bike: it's actually named the Streetfighter!

 **What do you and your friends think of streetfighters?**

## ONLINE//:

**http://www.Triumph.co.uk/usa/**
Click on Bikes/2011 Range for info on the Street Triple and the Street Triple R. You can even make your own Triumph motorcycle!

# *Bikes at Work*

**Many riders use motorcycles not just for fun but for their job. These include police, military** dispatch riders, paramedics, **and workers from auto association breakdown services.**

Harley-Davidson police motorcycles are popular in the United States.

# FF Top Fact

The best-known motorcycling charity is Riders for Health. It uses motorcycles to deliver vital healthcare to remote parts of Africa.

Bikes are also ridden by some medical workers. Motorcycling paramedics can often reach an accident to give help before an ambulance arrives. Motorcycles are often used to deliver blood and other medical supplies to hospitals.

The Honda Pan-European is reliable and fast.

## ONLINE//:

**http://www.riders.org**
Riders for Health uses motorcycles in Africa. Find out about their latest work on this site, plus click on the interactive map for detailed news.

# Sports Bikes

**Sports bikes are the fastest, most exciting machines on the road.**

Honda's Fireblade (below), Suzuki's GSX-R1000, and Yamaha's YZF-R1 (below right) have top speeds of more than 170 mph (275 km/h). Light **chassis** and road-gripping tires mean they can take corners fast, too.

## FF Top Fact

Most sports bikes have a fairing made from smooth plastic. This helps the bike cut through the air, making it faster and more controllable.

Many owners of sports bikes like to ride them on racetracks. Here they can ride fast with no traffic or speed limits. Some tracks have a racing school where riders can learn from **Grand Prix** stars.

## ONLINE//:

**http://www.sportrider.com**
Try the web site of magazine *Sport Rider* for cool bike tests and video clips in the Multimedia section.

# Superbike Racing

**The bikes used for Superbike racing are some of the world's fastest sports machines—tuned to make them even faster!**

Bikes must look like ordinary sports bikes, with only certain changes allowed. Yet the fastest Superbikes have top speeds of more than 185 mph (300 km/h).

# *FF* Record

British star Carl Fogarty won a record four Superbike championships for the Italian manufacturer Ducati—the most since the competition began in 1988.

Bikes used in the World Superbike championship include Ducati's 1198 (above), Honda's Fireblade, and Suzuki's GSX–R1000.

## ONLINE//:

**http://www.worldsbk.com**
Go to the official World Superbike site for the latest news and results, plus videos, free downloadables, and rider profiles.

# MotoGP

**The top level of motorcycle racing is MotoGP. This class is for pure racing machines. These are hand-built in very small numbers.**

MotoGP bikes are very powerful, light, and loud. Their tuned 49 cubic inches (800cc) engines make more than 200 **horsepower**. The bikes weigh less than 330 pounds (150 kg). Their exhausts are noisy.

This is the Yamaha M1 MotoGP bike.

At the Italian MotoGP, MotoGP bikes reach speeds of more than 198 mph (320 kph). This is faster than the speed a Boeing 747 jumbo jet takes off at.

# FF Top Fact

MotoGP racers cannot be ridden on the road. But in 2007, Ducati made a street-legal version of its MotoGP bike. The Desmosedici RR cost more than $63,000.

## ONLINE//:

**http://www.motogp.com**

Get onto this official MotoGP web site for the latest information and photos. Advisory: you have to pay to watch videos on this site.

# *Top Riders*

**Racing a motorcycle requires great skill and bravery. Top riders have the fastest bikes and are highly paid.**

Stars such as Casey Stoner, Leon Haslam, Valentino Rossi, and Noriyuki Haga race on circuits all around the world.

| | |
|---|---|
| Rider: | Casey Stoner |
| Country: | Australia |
| Nickname: | none |
| Racing class: | MotoGP |
| Bike: | Ducati Desmosedici |
| Best results: | MotoGP World Champion 2007 |
| Race number: | 27 |

| | |
|---|---|
| Rider: | Leon Haslam |
| Country: | UK |
| Nickname: | Pocket Rocket |
| Racing class: | World Superbike |
| Bike: | Honda Fireblade |
| Best results: | British Superbike championship, 2nd place 2006, 2008 |
| Race number: | 91 |

| Rider: | Valentino Rossi |
| --- | --- |
| Country: | Italy |
| Nickname: | The Doctor |
| Racing class: | MotoGP |
| Bike: | Yamaha YZR-M1 |
| Best results: | World Championship wins: 125cc 1997, 250cc 1999, 500cc 2001; MotoGP 2002–5, 2008–9 |
| Race number: | 46 |

| Rider: | Noriyuki Haga |
| --- | --- |
| Country: | Japan |
| Nickname: | Nitro Nori |
| Racing class: | World Superbike |
| Bike: | Ducati 1198 |
| Best results: | World Superbike championship, 2nd place 2000, 2007, 2009 |
| Race number: | 41 |

## ONLINE//:

http://www.yamaha-racing.com/Racing/motogp/rider_team/rossi.jsp

Valentino Rossi's web page on the Yamaha team web site.

# Off-Road Racing

**There are many different types of racing. One of the most exciting is motocross, in which fast, lightweight bikes zip around, not on roads but on a track that often includes big jumps.**

Many riders start motocross when they are young—some at just six years old.

Ricky Carmichael gets airbourne during the X Games 13. He won the gold medal.

# FF Record

American motocross hero Ricky Carmichael retired in 2008 after winning 16 championships and more than 150 races. His nickname was GOAT—Greatest Of All Time.

Enduros and rallies are tough off-road races that can last for days, or even weeks. The Dakar Rally in Africa takes place in a desert. Ice races take place in Russia and Sweden.

## ONLINE//:

**http://www.motocross.com**
The latest news from the motocross scene, including race and interview videos, image galleries, and bike reviews.

# Custom Bikes

**Custom bikes are specially designed and built by hand, so no two custom bikes are the same.**

Many have beautiful paintwork, shiny chrome, and other special details. They take a long time to build and are very expensive.

The best-known custom bikes are choppers. Most choppers have long forks, a big V-twin engine, a low seat, and a fat rear tire. TV shows such as *American Chopper* have made this type of bike very popular.

One of the most famous chopper builders is Arlen Ness from San Francisco—he's wearing the sunglasses. Arlen's hand-built bikes have won many custom shows. He runs a company making custom bikes and parts.

# FF Top Fact

The chopper from the movie *Easy Rider* is one of the most famous motorcycles ever built. The chopper below is a copy. The real one was destroyed in the making of the movie.

## ONLINE//:

**http://www.bdm.com**

Jaw-dropping web site of Big Dog Motorcycles. It includes their chopper models K-9, Pitball, and Wolf, and an online bike graphics book.

# Future Bikes

**Motorcycle manufacturers display their latest machines every year, at enormous shows in Italy, Germany, or Japan.**

Some of these, called concept bikes, are not ready to be sold. They show off ideas that might be used in years to come.

## FF Record

"Jamais Contente 2" is an electric bike from France. Powerful batteries helped it set a world record speed for an electric bike of more than 115 mph (185 km/h).

Jamais Contente 2 has a wraparound fairing to help it cut through the air.

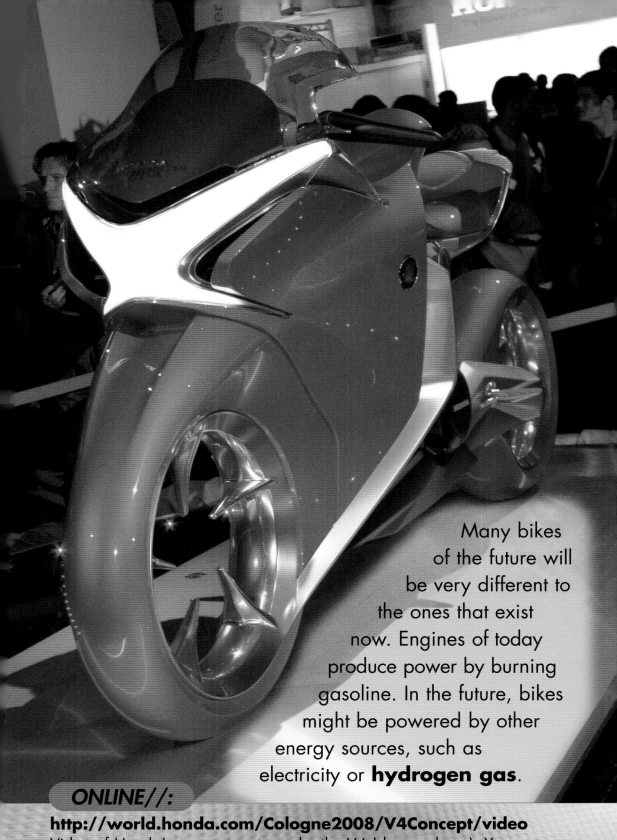

Many bikes of the future will be very different to the ones that exist now. Engines of today produce power by burning gasoline. In the future, bikes might be powered by other energy sources, such as electricity or **hydrogen gas**.

**ONLINE//:**
**http://world.honda.com/Cologne2008/V4Concept/video**
Video of Honda's concept motorcycle, the V4 (shown above). You can also find out about their latest releases and sports events from this page.

# *Answers*

**These are suggested answers to questions in this book. You may find that you have other answers. Talk about them with your friends. They may have other answers, too.**

**Page 5:** The answer to this question will depend on your own choices. You might want to ride a police motorcycle, so you can use the sirens to clear a path through traffic. Or you might prefer to ride an adventure bike across the desert.

**Page 11:** You might prefer a tourer for the added luxuries, such as the music system. You might like cruisers for the individual styling.

**Page 13:** You might like streetfighters for their aggressive looks, or you might hate them because you think they look ugly! See what your friends think.

# Glossary

**CC**—short for cubic centimeters, a unit of measurement used to show the size of an engine. Engine sizes are also given in cubic inches.

**Chassis**—the frame to which all parts of the bike are fixed.

**Class**—a group of bikes of the same type.

**Dispatch rider**—a person, usually in military service, whose job it is to deliver packages quickly.

**Fairing**—a shell on the front of some motorcycles that is shaped to reduce drag so the bike can cut through the air easily. Fairings help the bike travel faster.

**Grand Prix**—the top class of motor racing, or any top-class motorsport race.

**Horsepower**—a measurement of the power of an engine.

**Hydrogen gas**—a type of gas that could replace gasoline. It is much cleaner and does not cause pollution.

**Mph**—short for miles per hour, a measurement of distance traveled and the time taken. (Km/h means kilometers per hour.)

**Paramedic**—someone trained to give emergency medical help.

**Saddlebags**—bags to carry luggage, fitted on either side at the rear of the bike.

**Superbikes**—the fastest road bikes, and also the racing class for tuned-up road machines.

**Tuned**—modified or changed to improve performance, normally to make a bike faster.

**V-twin**—an engine with two cylinders that are arranged in a "V" shape.

**Wheelie**—riding with the bike's front wheel off of the ground. The wheelie is many riders' favorite trick!

# Index